William Shakespeare's Land of the Dead

A TRUE AND ACCURATE ACCOUNT
OF THE 1599 ZOMBIE PLAGUE

by John Heimbuch

A SAMUEL FRENCH ACTING EDITION

FOUNDED 1830

SAMUELFRENCH.COM

ISBN 978-0-573-70014-9   Printed in U.S.A.   #28099

MUSIC USE NOTE

Licensees are solely responsible for obtaining formal written permission from copyright owners to use copyrighted music in the performance of this play and are strongly cautioned to do so. If no such permission is obtained by the licensee, then the licensee must use only original music that the licensee owns and controls. Licensees are solely responsible and liable for all music clearances and shall indemnify the copyright owners of the play and their licensing agent, Samuel French, Inc., against any costs, expenses, losses and liabilities arising from the use of music by licensees.

IMPORTANT BILLING AND CREDIT REQUIREMENTS

All producers of *WILLIAM SHAKESPEARE'S LAND OF THE DEAD* must give credit to the Author of the Play in all programs distributed in connection with performances of the Play, and in all instances in which the title of the Play appears for the purposes of advertising, publicizing or otherwise exploiting the Play and/or a production. The name of the Author *must* appear on a separate line on which no other name appears, immediately following the title and *must* appear in size of type not less than fifty percent of the size of the title type.

In addition the following credit *must* be given in all programs and publicity information distributed in association with this piece:

William Shakespeare's Land of the Dead was originally produced by
Walking Shadow Theatre Company in the
2008 Minnesota Fringe Festival

WILLIAM SHAKESPEARE'S LAND OF THE DEAD was originally performed on August 2, 2008 at the Rarig Thrust Stage in Minneapolis during the Minnesota Fringe Festival. It was directed by Amy Rummenie and produced by Walking Shadow Theatre Company, with the following cast:

WILL KEMP	Craig Anderson
KATE BRAITHWAITE	Ariana Prusak
WILLIAM SHAKESPEARE	John Heimbuch
RICHARD BURBAGE	Keith Prusak
JOHN RICE	Michael Curran-Dorsano
JOHN SINKLO	David Pisa
FRANCIS BACON	Joseph Papke
SIR ROBERT CECIL	Shad Cooper
QUEEN ELIZABETH	Ellen Karsten
DOCTOR JOHN DEE	Jeff Huset
SOLDIER 1	Eric Zuelke
SOLDIER 2	Jen Zalar
AFFLICTED AND OTHERS	Christopher Bauleke, Jon Cole, Katherine Glover, Andrew Northrop, Valerie Rigsby, Erin Sheppard, Jennifer Walker

CHARACTERS

THE LORD CHAMBERLAIN'S MEN

WILLIAM SHAKESPEARE (35) – Player, playwright, company member
RICHARD BURBAGE (31) – Player and theatre manager
WILL KEMP (40s) – Player, clown, and Morris dancer
JOHN RICE (teens) – An apprentice player
KATE BRAITHWAITE (30s) – The attiring woman
JOHN SINKLO (30s) – A hired player

THE QUEEN'S COURT

FRANCIS BACON (38) – Lawyer, courier, philosopher
SIR ROBERT CECIL (36) – The Queen's spymaster
QUEEN ELIZABETH (65) – The Queen of England
DOCTOR JOHN DEE (71) – An astrologer and mathematician
SOLDIER 1 – A recruiting officer
SOLDIER 2 – A soldier of the Queen's guard

ADDITIONAL PLAYERS/SOLDIERS/AFFLICTED AS NEEDED

SETTING

Summer 1599. Southwark, England. In the tiring house of the newly built Globe Playhouse after the inaugural performance of William Shakespeare's *Henry the Fifth*.

"He that undertaketh the story of a time, especially of any length, cannot but meet with many blanks and spaces which he must be forced to fill up out of his own wit and conjecture."

- Francis Bacon,
The Advancement of Learning,
1620

For Matthew Kuzma and Katherine Fines

ACT I

DUSK

(The lights come up [LIGHT CUE 1] to reveal the backstage of the Globe playhouse – a candlelit changing room with a table, benches, and chairs, as well as chests, barrels, and baskets for storage. Littered around the tiring house are the costumes, props and weapons of Shakespeare's Henry the Fifth. *Entrances include a door leading outside, steps going upstairs, and a curtained alcove leading onto the playhouse stage - through which we hear Act V of* Henry the Fifth *being performed.)*

*(***WILL KEMP*** enters from the street. He is plainly dressed with Morris bells upon his legs. He listens to the performance.)*

*(***KATE*** enters with a wicker basket. She hears* **KEMP**, *but doesn't look up. She continues her chores.)*

KATE. Hallo, noisemaker! I can hear those bells stage left. And if it's young Master Rice, I'll thank you not to clatter the properties when you've an entrance to make.

KEMP. Never pass a chance to give a good scold, do you my Kate?

KATE. Will Kemp!

KEMP. Ah-haha! She lives, does she? My Katherine-Katherine-Kate. I wondered if Burbage would be kind enough to unscrew you from your sticking place when he tore down that decrepit Shoreditch pit they called the Theatre. But I see my little fixture has already been installed in the Globe.

KATE. What are you doing here? They'll be in the tiring house as soon as the play ends, and I doubt Master Shakespeare would be glad to see you. Today of all days.

KEMP. Shakerags can spit for all it's worth. I heard the talk all through London – Shakespeare's History of Henry the Fifth to open the Globe – so when I saw the banner raised today, I thought I'd see what he's done with my play now that Falstaff's not in it! And perchance give the good people a taste of what's missing.

KATE. Kemp, don't tell me you've come for a jig. Oh, God's wounds, you have.

KEMP. I confess 'twill be a touch jig-like. Behold in me the Nine Days Wonder!

KATE. Nine Days Wonder, what foolishness is that?

KEMP. Nay, ask not, but listen and be amazed!

KATE. You aren't going out there.

KEMP. You can be certain I am. At the end of part two did I not say Falstaff would return, by the playwright's own words? The Chamberlain's Men may be contentedly false, but I'll not let them make a liar of Kemp.

KATE. Will! This is no longer your Company and these not your roles! Shakespeare's already killed Falstaff off, what would he say if you barge onstage to grace his new Globe with your unwelcome legs?

KEMP. Don't think you'll thwart me my sweet Kate-o-nine tails. These unwelcome legs fought fraught Shoreditch streets to trod the boards - as all London talks of Irish wars and Spanish fleets. Even now I did yet 'scape a brawl. Near Surgeon's Hall I passed the rough remnant of an old tavern fight where some crazed jack-o-bedlam with blood-streaming lip and limbs all a-thrashing fell on me in fervor, but these true legs - which you would disparage - did bestow him such a kick that he collapsed on the street, whilst I, unscathed, did hie myself here to sit in a tavern over a middling cup of sack till that murderous William's two hours traffic had passed.

(A loud explosion is heard [SOUND CUE 1]. Like cannon-fire, or a nearby building collapsing.)

KATE. Now that's quite a sound!

KEMP. Was it not from the play?

KATE. No. Perhaps it was some regimental cannonry. There's a drill field nearby.

KEMP. Oh, there's an idea – let's build a playhouse in a marshy Southwark drill field. How very like Burbage. I bet the land was cheap. Who crosses the river to take in a play?

KATE. Well, I pray it desists.

KEMP. Pray a bit harder, else you may have to go tell the regiment that they disrupt a new play by Will Shakespeare. And failing that, bring it straight to the Queen.

KATE. I may do, if she persists to wage such noisome wars.

*('Onstage' the play draws to a close. As the actors bow, there is a burst of applause and stamping from the audience [SOUND CUE 2]. **KEMP** straightens his clothing.)*

KEMP. Hark the applause!

KATE. Kemp, I say don't!

KEMP. Alas dear Kate, my sweet-tongued shrew, these bells give me deafness to all but my cue - so till after my entrance I bid thee adieu!

*(**KEMP** greets the Lord Chamberlain's Men as they enter from the stage, including **BURBAGE**, the capable manager of the Chamberlain's Men, dressed as Hal; **RICE**, an apprentice player in his early teens, dressed as Katharine; and **SINKLO**, dressed as the King of France. Through the following, the Players remove their costumes and get dressed.)*

*(**SHAKESPEARE**, dressed as Burgundy/Chorus, enters last.)*

KEMP. My most notable Shakerags!

SHAKESPEARE. Kemp!

(KEMP *slides past* SHAKESPEARE *and heads onstage, where he begins to deliver his Nine Days Wonder speech.*)

BURBAGE. Shakespeare, leave him be.

SHAKESPEARE. Damn it, Burbage, what is he doing here?

KATE. He told me he was here to do a jig of sorts.

SHAKESPEARE. A jig!

BURBAGE. Kate.

SHAKESPEARE. And you didn't stop him?

KATE. Aye, there's a thought – stop Master Kemp once he's made up his mind. Stop him yourself if it matters to you. Master Sinkler, how many times must I ask you hired men not to throw your shirts on the floor?

BURBAGE. Will, I made it quite clear that Kemp not do a jig. A speech, nothing more.

SHAKESPEARE. You knew of this? And still you'd allow him to mar our inaugural show in the Globe, after what he's done?

BURBAGE. Oh please, Will, enough. We all know the cause. Kemp caught me in the Mermaid and asked to promote some wonder of his.

SHAKESPEARE. What wonder is this?

BURBAGE. Some dance or other, I saw no harm.

RICE. Is this Will Kemp the clown?

KATE. The same, Master John. Now be off with your wig.

RICE. I saw him play Falstaff and Bottom the Weaver. I thought he was funny.

SHAKESPEARE. Gather some years and you'll learn to feel different.

BURBAGE. Beware of your bite, William, the boy means no harm.

SHAKESPEARE. I needn't say more. Burbage can tell you just how comic Kemp is.

BURBAGE. Will.

KATE. They both have their gifts, no mistake, little John – but let this be proof, two strong Wills can never work well together.

SHAKESPEARE. It wouldn't be an issue if the damned prancing fool had just kept to the script. And when I kindly insisted that he stick to the page, he raised such a stink we had to cancel three shows!

BURBAGE. Look, Will. I barred him from playing, but I don't see the harm in promoting his work.

SHAKESPEARE. No? He's playing for Alleyn now! Imagine he discovered our prompt script, and brought it to Ned with Falstaff stuck back in it. What harm it would be if Ned Alleyn played your King Henry?

BURBAGE. Oh.

RICE. Could he do that?

SHAKESPEARE. Don't think he wouldn't.

KATE. He could but he won't.

SHAKESPEARE. You don't know Kemp as I do, my Kate.

KATE. It's still well enough. You may not like him, but that don't mean he's a thief.

SHAKESPEARE. See if he's not, Mistress Kate, and I will eat my words.

KATE. You certainly chew them enough.

BURBAGE. Will, there's nothing to gain by holding a grudge. We've both known Kemp since we had no beard – I think it only meet that we buy him a drink. All difference aside, he is still a friend.

(*A burst of laughter and applause from the stage [SOUND CUE 3].* **KEMP** *returns, dancing his way in.*)

KEMP. Aye, that'll give them a taste! And so my jig is up. Hey nonny good friends – some months hence and another bank of the Thames sees you all well met! A fine playhouse you've built. Sinklo, still hale as ever. Is that Condell and Heminges? – ah-ha! Hey, Burbage, my thanks – there's many now eager to see the Morris itself.

BURBAGE. Indeed, Kemp. I hope you are well.

KEMP. Oh, well enough. I'm playing with Ned again – courteous of him to have me back after all these years. Ah, you remember dear Shakes, how we played them back when Marlowe still held a pen? Why quiet, my glum little Shakestaff? I warn you now, silence is not so great a defense as you might suppose.

SHAKESPEARE. It's good to see you again, Kemp.

KEMP. Oh-ho, is that so, dear William the Second? And the same to you, if you say so. Now friends, let's drink your success in taking the Globe, may it please your creditors as much as it please you!

(The players cheer. They continue to change clothes.)

BURBAGE. Our creditors have every reason to be happy tonight!

KEMP. Not after we find the tavern, they won't. *(spookily)* They're coming to get you Burbage!

BURBAGE. Peace Kemp! I'll buy you that drink. To your great Morris and our new playhouse crowned by the reign of fierce Henry! Tonight at the Mermaid, the shareholders buy!

(The players cheer and react through the following.)

KEMP. Oh! Remind me, dear Shakes, after a draught, to bend your ear with an idea for a play.

SHAKESPEARE. Oh no, I fear I must beg off.

KEMP. Not in the least! You wrote this triumph, lacking though it may be in one noble knight.

SHAKESPEARE. Noble's hardly the word for what you had done! Jigging through the play, speaking to the audience, and running free with your words! No, Kemp. Falstaff died for thy sins, long before I scratched out his name. It could not be helped.

KEMP. But could you not at least show his death?

SHAKESPEARE. Forget not I had! A great hero's death in the battle of Shrewsbury. But like a base coward thou wouldst not stay dead, but rose resurrected, to say thou dissembled.

KEMP. Oh, and was there not a laugh? The best ever heard! Laughed so hard that you begged me to keep it and then penned it in. Did you not pen it in?

SHAKESPEARE. Yes.

KEMP. Then scold not me! Oh how they roared to hear us played! We had them that day, and so they returned for part two! And so we said it would be with Hal Five. Good fights, strong princes, and Falstaff for laughs. And where was the truth in that? No Falstaff today! The audience comes, when they do, to see an actor play a role. Not for the words but for the clowning, jesting, speaking, acting, singing, jigging, fighting best of us. The words in the play are but fine trimmings on our effort.

SHAKESPEARE. Is that so?

KEMP. Aye, by my tongue, so it is!

SHAKESPEARE. Then I must thank you, Kemp, for telling me so. In my folly I thought that some might have come to hear a story, but now I see: they're here for thee, Kemp, and any praise that I receive is a mere fool's fancy.

KEMP. At least now you know. You should be grateful to me, Shakerags, for whom else could make thy Dogberry, Falstaff, and Bottom ring true, but one Cavaliero Kemp - who with wit and jig did send thy words to the heights of Olympus!

SHAKESPEARE. May God grace thee for it, Kemp, for I know I cannot. But what of Mistress Katherine?

KATE. Nay, bring me not in this.

KEMP. Yes, do Shakes, make sense.

SHAKESPEARE. How couldst thou play thy roles without her pins? 'Twas she made Bottom into a perfect ass and padded Falstaff's glutton's belly with special hose. She sewed thy buttons, polished thy bells, and oft did make a motley fool of thee. So tell me, dear Kemp, if you will, how is it a player may thrive without stage, nor words, nor clothes of any kind?

KEMP. If he be skilled enough a man can earn his bread by dance alone. Hence the Nine Days Wonder!

SHAKESPEARE. What wonder is this?

KEMP. To dance a Morris from London to Norwich!

SHAKESPEARE. London to Norwich in nine days? That's madness.

KEMP. Well, they aren't nine days in a row! Or how could I savor my fame in each town on the way?

SHAKESPEARE. A fine fool's idea.

KEMP. No wonder. It's yours.

SHAKESPEARE. Mine?

KEMP. Yes! Do you not recall that you bid me to dance if I wouldn't play as you bade? Well, at first I gnashed my teeth over your suggestion, but then Sinklo called it a fine idea, and I thought here's my final chance to turn your words to my gain. So you see: to play a fool is not to be a fool. Nine Days dancing will bring more than a year in the Chamberlain's Men!

SHAKESPEARE. Then go dance thy Nine Men's Morris, I wish thee the best.

KEMP. Now that's a first - William Shakespeare wishes Will Kemp the best! There's a fine one. I'll best you! I'll best the great lot of you over a good pot of ale! A-ha! To the tavern with all!

(The players cheer. **KEMP** *and the players exit, leaving* **BURBAGE, SHAKESPEARE, RICE,** *and* **KATE.***)*

BURBAGE. Will you not bury your hatchet?

SHAKESPEARE. I would bury it in him. But by all means, go in good faith. Drink with him a pot of ale, and say what thou wilt of me. I'm sure there's much to say.

BURBAGE. You're sure you won't join us?

SHAKESPEARE. No. I am in pain.

BURBAGE. John?

RICE. By and by, once I'm unmade.

BURBAGE. Indeed, at the tavern it's wise to be less a maid than you now seem. Kate?

KATE. Nay Richard, my only, the banner will not bring itself in. But with my blessing, you may give this to Kemp.

(**KATE** *kisses* **BURBAGE**.)

BURBAGE. I'd rather keep it myself, lest the intent be lost in the conveyance.

KATE. As you please.

BURBAGE. It would please me to please you.

KATE. Aye, 'tis well known – go on, your fellows await.

BURBAGE. So they do. Good night to you all!

(**BURRBAGE** *exits to the street*.)

SHAKESPEARE. Well Master Rice, you've played your first role.

RICE. I'm sorry if I offended, sir.

SHAKESPEARE. No, John – yours is not the apology I seek. Did you enjoy playing Katherine?

RICE. I enjoyed speaking your words.

SHAKESPEARE. We'll see if you still feel the same once you've said a few more of them. How came you to the playhouse?

RICE. By the river.

SHAKESPEARE. An apprentice wit as well, I see. I meant, how came you to your apprenticeship.

RICE. And as I said, by the river. My father's a boatman, and saw the Globe being built. When the Queen began to conscript against the Irish Rebellion, he said: "If you must serve the crown by playing a soldier, I'd rather it was in the playhouse than the field." Watermen's sons are oft pressed to service.

SHAKESPEARE. You ever pilot a bark?

RICE. Wouldn't be a boatman's boy if I hadn't. Sir, how came you to acting?

SHAKESPEARE. My father's a glover. He sat in the guildhall at Stratford where the traveling players performed till some strife over sympathies encouraged him to sign me to Ned Alleyn's company.

KATE. His father's a catholic.

SHAKESPEARE. Kate!

KATE. Is he not?

SHAKESPEARE. Leave it be.

RICE. And were you there with Will Kemp?

SHAKESPEARE. Long ago. We were once good friends.

KATE. Young master John, take this to heart: No actor of skill, no matter how great, is ever the better to fight with a playwright.

RICE. Why?

KATE. Because playwrights fight dirty. Any thing that you say may be put on the stage to paint a sad mockery of you.

RICE. But you've not done this of Kemp?

KATE. Hasn't he, now? I'm sure some work of betrayal has even this moment been set to the page. Do tell us, Will - what is your next play?

SHAKESPEARE. It's not about Kemp.

KATE. So it's a betrayal, is it?

SHAKESPEARE. Perhaps. Oh, now you'll laugh.

KATE. Come now, the title!

SHAKESPEARE. The Tragedy of Julius Caesar.

KATE. A ha! What did I say – a betrayal! And what a betrayal it is.

SHAKESPEARE. I knew you would laugh.

KATE. Oh Will, how you worry. We all know you're brilliant. See how the hairline withdraws to make room for the brain!

RICE. Master Shakespeare, can all men be so found in their art?

SHAKESPEARE. Art is an echo of the person who made it. But you need an astute ear indeed to locate its source. If a man wished know me, he'd be much better served to buy me a pint.

RICE. And how will they know you a hundred years hence?

SHAKESPEARE. If my work is still known a hundred years hence, I'll buy you that pint.

RICE. Don't think they'll endure?

SHAKESPEARE. Plays are nothing but a product of their times, likely to wane with the fashion of the day. No, Master Rice, if anything it is by the strength of the youth that our art shall survive. So be attentive and studious, and the length of your days shall be the legacy of mine.

RICE. With any luck, I'll be out of this dress before those days end.

SHAKESPEARE. Ha!

KATE. Don't you encourage him.

SHAKESPEARE. No no, of course. You see, Master John, for all my dark sonnets, Kate knows me too well.

KATE. I know Burbage better. They may be your words, but he brings them to life.

SHAKESPEARE. Good thing he does, my wife wouldn't approve.

KATE. Do you think that his does?

SHAKESPEARE. I try not to wonder. Have you ever told him?

KATE. Oh, zounds, Will. What's past is past.

SHAKESPEARE. He's still my best friend.

KATE. And need I remind you that you called it off? There's nothing to tell. He's happy not knowing and I'm glad he doesn't. Telling him now would only spell trouble. You're both married men - with daughters, I might add. I'm sorry –

SHAKESPEARE. Please don't. Will you never wed?

KATE. Be glad that I don't. Then where would you be? You lot can't even pick up your costumes, let alone unlace a corset.

RICE. Speaking of, Mistress Kate –

KATE. Now for that you must wait, Master Rice.

(There is a knock on the exterior door.)

SHAKESPEARE. If that's some well-wisher, I've gone out.

KATE. Yes, yes.

(KATE *opens the door to* FRANCIS BACON. *He is an exceedingly well-dressed lawyer and advisor to Queen Elizabeth. He is in his late 30s, with a stately beard and an air of conscious superiority.*)

KATE. Good evening, sir.

BACON. Madam, if Master Shakespeare is within tell him that Francis Bacon would share a word.

KATE. Alas, Master Bacon, Shakespeare has gone for the night.

SHAKESPEARE. Francis Bacon, you say?

KATE. Aye, but 'tis pointless for me to tell him you've gone when you shout his name so!

(SHAKESPEARE *goes to the door, greeting* BACON.)

SHAKESPEARE. Master Bacon, a pleasure to see you outside the Queen's court.

BACON. Master Shakespeare, do you always tell your servants to turn away gentlemen of breeding?

SHAKESPEARE. No, of course. Thank you, Kate.

(KATE *gives* SHAKESPEARE *a look and returns to her chores.*)

SHAKESPEARE. Master Bacon, an honor. I must thank you again for the gift of your essays last winter at Richmond. Such well-formed thoughts, so concisely put.

BACON. Yes.

SHAKESPEARE. And, uh, what brings you to visit the Lord Chamberlain's Men?

BACON. Why, to see the new Globe, of course! 'tis a wonderful building with a good view of the river – although the magic does wear off somewhat backstage.

SHAKESPEARE. Oh. Our apprentice, John Rice. Francis Bacon.

(RICE *curtseys. Then bows. Unsure.*)

RICE. Did you enjoy Henry the Fifth, sir?

BACON. You know, the problem with a new playhouse is that they're always more entertaining than the plays they contain. Oh this one was decent enough. Cleverness, fighting. Burbage was good. Though I couldn't help but notice that Jack Falstaff was missing.

SHAKESPEARE. The problems with Falstaff were out of my hands.

BACON. A shame. May we speak in private?

(SHAKESPEARE looks at KATE.)

KATE. John, go upstairs.

RICE. I would prefer to go to the tavern.

KATE. Young man, I must first sweep the stage, bolt the doors and bring down the banner.

RICE. But -

KATE. – But me no buts. The whole riverside needn't think we're doing a show when we aren't. Your corset shall wait. Upstairs, now.

RICE. Then 'tis on your head if my hem should catch on the step.

KATE. Go. Sirs, by your leave.

(RICE exits upstairs. KATE exits onto the stage.)

SHAKESPEARE. Sir, I am at your service. I hope it nothing serious.

BACON. Quite serious, yes.

SHAKESPEARE. Some legal matter, is it?

BACON. Master Shakespeare, though we barely spoke at Richmond, in plain terms I am a tremendous enthusiast for your work. I've seen most of your plays a couple times each, read and re-read the poems by your hand, and built a good sense of your qualities as an author. The lyricism, the form and phrase of your thoughts, there's a voice in your work not unlike my own. A finesse, if you will.

SHAKESPEARE. Oh. Um. Thank you, sir.

BACON. I have an idea for a play that I think you might like.

SHAKESPEARE. I'm happy to hear it, but I'm only the playwright. Any new play must be submitted to Burbage. He'll pay ten pounds for the script if he likes it enough.

BACON. Ten pounds! How can a play command such a price?

SHAKESPEARE. The Lord Chamberlain's Men have a grant for new work.

BACON. From whom?

SHAKESPEARE. The Lord Chamberlain.

BACON. Well, if you'll allow me, I don't think it's yet ready for Burbage. I wish for a play to commemorate the Queen's Order of the Garter.

SHAKESPEARE. Garnishing favor?

BACON. While Essex fights the Irish, my hands are tied at court. But a play's the means to catch the conscience of the Queen. If it could return me to her counsel, I would gladly commission thee for it.

SHAKESPEARE. Commission me?

BACON. How's thirty pounds?

SHAKESPEARE. Tell me this play. The setting?

BACON. Windsor.

SHAKESPEARE. A pastoral!

BACON. It's more an idyll of country town life.

SHAKESPEARE. It's less idyllic than you'd think. What is the premise?

BACON. An old knight goes a-wooing, and the wives of the town do play several tricks upon him.

SHAKESPEARE. Why? Are they angry?

BACON. No, they're quite merry.

SHAKESPEARE. I see. Tell me more.

BACON. Where was I?

SHAKESPEARE. With these merry wives of Windsor. Is there a title?

BACON. Oh, you'll love this! I call it *Falstaff in Love!*

SHAKESPEARE. That's a... fine name.

BACON. I knew you would like it.

SHAKESPEARE. - except that Falstaff is dead.

BACON. So bring him back. Thirty pounds for thy pains.

SHAKESPEARE. Hardly enough to bring a man back to life.

BACON. Call it forty then.

SHAKESPEARE. Master Bacon –

BACON. Fifty!

SHAKESPEARE. If you're so particular about what it contains, why don't you simply write it?

BACON. Well, as it happens.

(**BACON** *pulls out a sheaf of handwritten pages. A pause.*)

SHAKESPEARE. Now I'm confused. You want to commission a play that you've already written?

BACON. As the Queen's legal counsel, I shouldn't write a play.

SHAKESPEARE. So strike off your name.

BACON. Burbage might still refuse it.

SHAKESPEARE. Rejection's a risk that all playwrights face.

BACON. But with your name on the page it's assured a production.

SHAKESPEARE. Well, it is my playhouse, after all.

BACON. Besides, there's no merit in an anonymous commission. But William Shakespeare's *Falstaff in Love*, now that's a prize! And already written to suit my needs.

SHAKESPEARE. And what of my needs? Like consistency. I can't just bring Falstaff back. The dear knight is dead, and will not revive. Or should I ignore the whole plot of my *Henry the Fifth*?

(*There is a pounding, scratching sound on the outside door.*)

BACON. Well I didn't think you'd kill him off when I wrote it.

SHAKESPEARE. Authors sometimes do that.

BACON. Perhaps it could occur before your *Henry the Fourth*.

SHAKESPEARE. Kate, the door! Fine. Let's suppose it does, will Prince Hal join him in Windsor?

BACON. Oh no, Hal can't be there. It celebrates the Queen.

SHAKESPEARE. Now, how can it occur before the two Henry plays and still celebrate our queen? Had Falstaff not died when Hal was crowned, he'd be a mere two hundred and fifty years old!

BACON. Master Shakespeare, I'd hope that you of all men would allow a little imagination in your art.

(**RICE** *enters, still in his dress.*)

RICE. Shall I get the door?

SHAKESPEARE. Not as you're dressed – go and get Kate.

(*Beat.* **RICE** *goes to get* **KATE**.)

SHAKESPEARE. Let me be clear on this point, Master Bacon, to be art it must be truthful.

BACON. Truthful! There's a laugh! Boys dressed as women dressed as men? Fairy kings and queens? Two sets of long-lost twins from different places with the same improbable names? Are these the trappings of truth?

SHAKESPEARE. There is a truth to them. Truth in art is different than truth in life.

BACON. Oh, you think I don't know this? I practiced your craft with Kit Marlowe when we were both at Grey's Inn.

SHAKESPEARE. And see where that got him.

BACON. Christopher Marlowe would have done well to keep his mouth shut and do what was asked of him.

SHAKESPEARE. What does that mean?

BACON. Only that I suggest thou learn from his mistakes, and show a healthy respect for thy superiors, Master Shakespeare. Truth in politics is different than truth in life – I hope thy plays are not more conscious of that fact than thee.

SHAKESPEARE. And what if you should later claim it as your own? Might not all of my plays then suffer confusion, till none knew whether 'twas Shakespeare or Bacon who wrote them?

BACON. Anyone might make such a claim! Imagine if the Earl of Oxford said the same.

SHAKESPEARE. Edward De Vere is not a Star Chamber lawyer who serves the Queen's court. I think there's no question whose word bears more weight, yours or mine.

(**KATE** and **RICE** return.)

KATE. ...so the banner must wait, must it? No mistake, Master John, when men talk business they don't lift a finger.

(**KATE** opens the door, revealing **SINKLO**. He looks more unwell than usual.)

KATE. Aye, Master Sinklo – what brings you back?

(**SINKLO** starts to speak but collapses instead. And twitches.)

KATE. Now, is that any way to behave?

SHAKESPEARE. What, drunk already?

RICE. He's bleeding.

SHAKESPEARE. Well, get him up... Master Bacon, forgive him. After an opening performance some celebration is normal. Today much sooner than usual.

BACON. Are all your players so debauched?

SHAKESPEARE. No, just most of them. I thought they were going to the Mermaid.

KATE. I'd say he found the bearpit, by the look of him. Master Sinckler, arise. John, don't soil that dress.

SHAKESPEARE. Kate, lead him out. He looks unwell.

BACON. I really should go.

SHAKESPEARE. Stay but a moment.

RICE. Wait, he's not –

(KATE *tries to help* SINKLO *up, but when she touches him he enters some sort of fervor.* SINKLO *bites* KATE *on the arm. Hard.*)

KATE. AAHHHH!

SHAKESPEARE. Kate!

KATE. GOOD GOD!!! Get him off! I say get him off!

RICE. Stop him! Oh murder!

SHAKESPEARE. Good Christ almighty! Sinklo, let go!

(BACON *draws his sword.*)

BACON. Desist I say, in the name of the Queen!

(RICE *clubs* SINKLO *with a theatrical prop.* SINKLO *releases his bite and snarls at* RICE.)

BACON. Stand down!

RICE. Help her, she's hurt!

SHAKESPEARE. John!

BACON. Stand down, I say!

(SINKLO *charges* RICE. BACON *knocks* RICE *aside and stabs* SINKLO, *who dies on the sword and falls to the ground.*)

SHAKESPEARE. Are you bleeding?

KATE. Don't touch me!

SHAKESPEARE. John, go and get water! Go.

(RICE *goes out.*)

SHAKESPEARE. Does he live?

BACON. There's no breath in him.

SHAKESPEARE. What possessed him to do this?

KATE. I can't feel my fingers.

SHAKESPEARE. It's simply the pain. They'll come back in good time. Don't tense your arm. Can you cut a bandage?

(BACON *picks up a piece of clothing.*)

KATE. Not the good robe! Use the chemise.

(**BACON** *picks up different piece of clothing. He tears out a strip.*)

SHAKESPEARE. Sit quiet now, Kate.

BACON. That wound is severe.

SHAKESPEARE. It will at least be well-bound. Hold this a moment, it has to be taut.

BACON. In truth, I can't stay.

SHAKESPEARE. No, but you must! They'll close down the Globe unless you tell them what happened!

BACON. Oh I'm sure this sort of thing occurs all the time in Southwark. He wasn't a company member, was he?

SHAKESPEARE. No. Just a hired man.

BACON. Good, then pay the family his stipend and call it concluded.

(**RICE** *re-enters.*)

SHAKESPEARE. Where's the water?

RICE. The riverfront's swarmed. People in droves are crossing the Thames, some are wounded, all are wet, and a great many soldiers stand at the ready. Downriver is thick with debris. The barks cannot pass. Word is the plague.

BACON. Ah yes, enjoy your new playhouse! And I hope you don't mind if as Queen's Counsel, I offer this bit of pro bono advice: Don't mention my name.

SHAKESPEARE. But you've killed an actor!

BACON. And think of how poorly that would reflect upon me. Besides, you can explain better than I, Master Shakespeare. You have a way with words.

(**BURBAGE** *arrives from outside.*)

BURBAGE. Will, thank God you're here! The streets are pure madness! The bridge has collapsed.

BACON. Collapsed?

SHAKESPEARE. That will bring a drop in attendance.

BURBAGE. Did Sinklo come back here? He fell back in the press approaching the river.

SHAKESPEARE. There he is. And much gaunter than usual.

BURBAGE. What in God's name?

SHAKESPEARE. He was wounded when he arrived and collapsed at the threshold. Master Bacon, of course, hath witnessed all.

RICE. Master Shakespeare –

BURBAGE. Yes, Master Bacon, of course. Will, is he...?

BACON. He is dead, Master Burbage.

BURBAGE. No.

KATE. Richard – ah!

BURBAGE. Kate, are you well?

RICE. She was hurt in the fight.

KATE. A scratch, nothing more.

BURBAGE. What fight?

SHAKESPEARE. Some ruffians came in from the street, but Master Bacon fended them off. We owe him our lives.

BACON. Yes, though I'm afraid I can't stay.

BURBAGE. But you must be our witness.

BACON. That depends on some factors, does it not, Master Shakespeare?

SHAKESPEARE. It will earn you my thanks, and all that it means.

BACON. Then I'll do what I can.

BURBAGE. Many thanks, sir. I'm grateful to you that our dear Kate is safe. Are you in pain?

KATE. I am oddly cold. But give it some time, it hurts less already.

BURBAGE. I'm just glad you're safe.

(They kiss. **KEMP** *and the other players return.)*

KEMP. ...so it seems we must locate a more local tavern. - Oh, Burbage you devil! - What's happened to Sinklo?

SHAKESPEARE. A touch of misfortune has left him quite dead.

KEMP. Well, that's some ill news. I leave the players and all hell breaks loose.

BURBAGE. Kemp. Leave it be.

KEMP. You're one to talk! Your Southwark playhouse has cost him his life, and what do you do? Go tend to your minx, he wasn't your friend.

BURBAGE. Alright Kemp. Ha ha. You have me.

KATE. *(in sudden pain)* Master Kemp, do you call me a whore?

BURBAGE. Please, Kate, it's only a jest.

KATE. A serious one; and what do you do? I toil each day to wash your bright colors and mend up your hose, and what thanks? Two calloused hands and these dim-growing eyes. No applause for your Kate – just a tuppence a day and these disgusting right dogs of the stage, always barking "Kate! Kate! Kate!"

RICE. I don't bark at you.

KATE. Oh no, Master Rice. You're new to the role, but I'm sure you'll prove a quick study.

BURBAGE. What causes this?

SHAKESPEARE. Aye, peace, Katherine – you are wounded.

KATE. Oh, not so wounded in my body as my pride, but what's pride to you? You'd support any monarch who gives you a coin, but I know the truth. What would your family say? That you celebrate Essex with this play of yours, for quelling the Irish at the edge of his sword all so good Queen Bess can slaughter her Catholics. I would she would join them, the merciless bitch.

BURBAGE. Kate, please. Francis Bacon is the Queen's counsel.

KATE. I don't give a fart what he is to our heretic Queen. I pray the Spanish arrive like the Romans to conquer this barbarous England and return us to the faith of our fathers.

KEMP. Be still your tongue.

SHAKESPEARE. She knows not what she says –

KATE. Do I not? At the chapel in Stratford did you not say "Behind this white wall is painted good Saint George, awaiting true England like the Avalon King"?

SHAKESPEARE. I'll have no part in this treason.

KATE. My head, how it swims!

BURBAGE. Kate.

KATE. Enough, leave me be!

(**KATE** *runs upstairs with growing difficulty.*)

SHAKESPEARE. Please, Master Bacon, I must ask you to pay her no heed.

BACON. Is this true? Are you a Catholic?

SHAKESPEARE. You know I am not.

BACON. When I speak to the courts, I will strive to be reasoned.

BURBAGE. You won't report her?

BACON. I am a crown lawyer, Master Burbage. That may not mean much to you, but it does to me. Between rebellion in Ireland and the Spanish Armada, I am obliged to report any Catholic threat, no matter how small. Now if you'll excuse me, I must cross the Thames.

BURBAGE. Oh, could this day be any worse?

(**BACON** *goes to open the door, but he barely reaches the handle when it flies open and the room floods with* **AFFLICTED** – *frenzied men and women, covered in blood, who move with extreme difficulty. They attack with a clawing, biting aggression.*)

(*All fight. It should be realistic and horrifying, with lots of screaming, shouting, and confusion. Ad-libbing is encouraged, provided it doesn't drown out any subsequent dialogue.*)

BACON. Ahh!

BURBAGE. What are they?

KEMP. The devil, I say!? Get back!

RICE. They've gone mad like Sinklo!

BURBAGE. Ah! Off! Be off! A sword!

KEMP. Help! They're upon me!

SHAKESPEARE. Kemp, away with those bells! Have we no real weapons?

BURBAGE. Why the devil would we want real weapons onstage?

SHAKESPEARE. This serves us right for skimping on authenticity!

(*More shouting and snarling as the fight continues. The extra players are bitten and killed. They rise as afflicted.*)

KEMP. They rise again!

BACON. It's the bite.

BURBAGE. What?

BACON. They rise from the bite! Beware their bite!

(*More shouting. At the apex of the battle* **KEMP, BURBAGE, SHAKESPEARE, BACON,** *and* **RICE** *are unbitten but outnumbered. Things look grim, when...*)

SOLDIER. (*outside*) Ho! Within! Stand for the Queen.

(**SOLDIERS** *rush in and fight the afflicted. The remaining players assist as they are able.*)

BURBAGE. Who are they?

BACON. Soldiers for the queen.

KEMP. Timely bastards!

SHAKESPEARE. From whence came they?

KEMP. Can you not speak normal, for once?

(*Together they kill off the afflicted. Everyone still has weapons drawn. Neither the players nor the soldiers quite trust each other.*)

SOLDIER. Are all that still stand men?

BURBAGE. All are sir.

KEMP. (*of* **RICE**) Even this one, though he may not appear it.

SOLDIER 2. Lord Cecil! It's clear!

BACON. Robert Cecil is here?

SOLDIER 2. Sir.

BACON. Then we are saved!

(**ROBERT CECIL** *enters. A military-minded man with great authority. He moves with slight difficulty. He surveys the carnage.*)

CECIL. Clear the dead from this room.

BACON. Robert Cecil! You are well met in Southwark.

(**BACON** *approaches* **CECIL.** *They clasp arms.*)

CECIL. Ah, Francis, yours is a welcome face. Is this the new Globe? You must be the Chamberlain's Men.

BURBAGE. It is and we are, my Lord.

KEMP. Or what remains of them anyway.

BURBAGE. My lord, I am Burbage. This is Rice, Shakespeare, and Kemp.

SHAKESPEARE. – who has since left the company.

CECIL. You know, Master Bacon, there's a rumor at court that you have some hand with these players.

SHAKESPEARE. Completely unfounded.

BACON. As he says.

CECIL. Nevertheless, the Queen will be pleased.

BACON. The Queen, is she – ?

CECIL. With us and well. She was in Richmond when the unrest began. We set five boats downriver to bring her to safety. But as we saw the remains of London Bridge, I knew the affliction had spread. I put the entire company ashore near the Tower where we were quickly overrun. The few that escaped met a band of recruiters and together piloted the Queen's bark to Southwark. We saw your banner. You see what remains. Are there others within?

BURBAGE. None that still live, except our tiring girl, Kate.

CECIL. And all unafflicted?

BURBAGE. My lord, I don't know.

CECIL. Trust me, you would. How strong is your playhouse?

BURBAGE. New built with good lumber.

CECIL. For the moment 'twill serve.

RICE. So we are safe?

CECIL. Ha! My boy, safety is naught but a mountebank's trick, a deceitful illusion one can never believe. At best we have bought some time to prepare and defend ourselves. You have weapons?

BURBAGE. Stage weapons only, dulled and barbed for our plays.

CECIL. Unbarb them. They shall soon be in much demand.

BURBAGE. Forgive me, my Lord, but what the devil is going on? What is this?

CECIL. This is a plague of maddening bloodlust, bringing ferocity and death, though not in that order.

BURBAGE. Meaning?

CECIL. That times have been that when the brains were out, the man would die, and there an end; but now they rise again.

BACON. Have you determined the cause?

CECIL. None can be sure. John Dee says that demons attack the soul through an imbalance of the humours.

BACON. John Dee is a fool.

CECIL. He's here with the Queen. *(to a soldier)* Go, bid them in.

BACON. Oh. Won't that be fun. Have any of your men succumbed?

CECIL. Several.

BACON. And had they been bitten?

CECIL. We all have been bitten.

BACON. All?

CECIL. Most of us, anyhow. Not the Queen and not Dee, and one or two of the men. But we've been fighting all day and most are now wounded, though I assure you, not badly.

BACON. And you, Robert?

CECIL. *(showing a bite mark)* As you see.

BACON. Then I must ask a favor. Forgive me, but those unbitten must stay with the Queen. The rest must patrol the playhouse grounds, and secure all the gates.

BURBAGE. Master Bacon, the playhouse is locked for the night.

BACON. Then they must check the locks. Upstairs is a woman who can show them the grounds. Have them bring her down.

BURBAGE. With all respect, Master Bacon -

BACON. She is wounded, and won't wish to comply, but I tell you she must. Enforce it however you will.

BURBAGE. No, this is madness!

BACON. Yet there is method in it. I promise you.

CECIL. You are in earnest.

BACON. Upon my life, Robert, I have never been more so.

(*Enter* **QUEEN ELIZABETH** – *an aging but still beautiful monarch, with a wit so dry it can start fires. She is escorted by soldiers. All bow. Deeply.*)

CECIL. Welcome, your Majesty.

QUEEN ELIZABETH. What place is this?

CECIL. The Globe Playhouse, your majesty. I hope you will find it suitable.

QUEEN ELIZABETH. I'm quite certain I won't - to be confined within this player's palace, like some common thief, vagabond or cur. I had rather be confined to the bear pit, for at least those great brutes are wiser than to fawn and curtsy so. If your father were still alive, I would never have to stoop so low.

CECIL. Yes, your majesty.

QUEEN ELIZABETH. That's even lower than you, my pygmy.

CECIL. Thank you, your Majesty. May I?

QUEEN ELIZABETH. Do as you must.

(*All rise.*)

CECIL. Men, who amongst you is yet unwounded?

SOLDIER 1. I am, my lord.

SOLDIER 2. And I as well.

CECIL. Good. Stay you both with the Queen. The rest will patrol the exterior wall. Upstairs is a woman. Go and fetch her. She will escort you, however unwillingly. Go.

(*Some soldiers exit upstairs to fetch* **KATE.**)

BURBAGE. Wait –

SHAKESPEARE. Mind yourself, Richard.

BACON. My Queen, it a great relief to see you here.

QUEEN ELIZABETH. I'm glad at least one of us feels that way, Master Bacon. Master Shakespeare, this is your playhouse?

SHAKESPEARE. It is, my liege, in part.

QUEEN ELIZABETH. I must admit, the pile of corpses was a bit unexpected, but very appropriate. I now begin to see where you draw your inspiration.

(**KEMP** *laughs.*)

QUEEN ELIZABETH. Master Kemp, are you amused?

KEMP. Ahem. Your generosity, my Queen, in matters of wit, proves 'tis better to give than receive.

QUEEN ELIZABETH. I would not know otherwise. In all my munificence, none has the courage to give back to me.

(**DOCTOR DEE** *enters.*)

DOCTOR DEE. Your Majesty, have you seen! There's fire beyond the Thames, soon all of London will be aflame.

QUEEN ELIZABETH. Ah, Doctor Dee. That is a relief. I was beginning to worry.

DOCTOR DEE. You needn't more, for by God's grace you're safe in the Globe – and not deposed by the madness that lives within the minds of your subjects, whose bilious humors grow rank, inducing their minds to a torporous state of bloodlust, until they are so lacking in the sanguinary element that they must seek it in the flesh of others -

QUEEN ELIZABETH. Yes yes yes. My dear Doctor - I sent thee to serve as a Dean in Manchester so I would not have to hear thy incessant hand-wringing. Why must I listen to it now?

DOCTOR DEE. I am on leave for the summer. Manchester is a dismal unkind place, your Majesty. They call me a sorcerer, and say I convene with spirits.

QUEEN ELIZABETH. But, my dear Dee, you do convene with spirits.

DOCTOR DEE. That is no matter.

KEMP. No matter indeed! Why 'tis the very lack of matter that makes them spirits.

QUEEN ELIZABETH. Too right, Master Kemp.

(*The* **SOLDIERS** *enter, dragging* **KATE** *with them.*)

KATE. I say leave me be!

BACON. Kate - that is her name?

SHAKESPEARE. Yes.

BACON. Lord Cecil needs someone who can show these men the playhouse grounds. Can you do that?

KATE. I am unwell.

BACON. But I know you'll be strong. For your Queen.

BURBAGE. You can't ask this. She's wounded. I'll go.

BACON. No. I say she will go. Robert Cecil will protect her.

CECIL. I bear the marks. I'll do what I must. By my sword, Master Burbage, I will protect her.

BURBAGE. You can't mean this.

BACON. I assure you I do.

BURBAGE. Your Majesty, please - !

QUEEN ELIZABETH. My dear Burbage, though Francis Bacon may be a sycophant, I have often found that in matters of logic, it is best to trust his counsel.

BACON. Escort her outside.

(*The bitten soldiers escort* **KATE** *outside.*)

KATE. No! Richard!

BURBAGE. Kate!

(**SHAKESPEARE** *stops* **BURBAGE.**)

CECIL. Your Majesty.

QUEEN ELIZABETH. Go in good faith, my dear pygmy.

(*The* **QUEEN** *extends her hand.* **CECIL** *kisses it.*)

CECIL. My Queen, it is an honor. Until my return, Master Bacon shall be your protector.

QUEEN ELIZABETH. (*under her breath*) Oh god.

CECIL. Be wise in this, Francis.

BACON. I shall, my friend.

(*They clasp hands.* **CECIL** *hugs* **BACON.**)

BACON. To better times.

CECIL. Many thanks. Men, lock and bar the door behind us! We will knock thrice and thrice upon our return. Beware the afflicted!

(**CECIL** *draws his sword and exits. The two unbitten soldiers bar the door.*)

BACON. They will not knock.

BURBAGE. What good does it do to just throw them out, you unconscionable ass!

BACON. I'm all for doing good, but blind help won't help anyone. They have been bitten, as are all we have seen who succumb. Induction would hold that the afflicted are bitten. While I cannot advocate killing them, neither can I advocate anything that will help seal our doom.

DOCTOR DEE. The bite brings affliction?

BACON. Yes.

BURBAGE. But putting them out to die?

BACON. What evidence is there that our help can save her? None. It simply absolves your guilt. When facing such dangers, it is best for us all to be well-reasoned! If I were so bitten, I hope you'd do the same.

DOCTOR DEE. My Queen, from Richmond to here, I believe there is in the spread of this affliction a mathematic that will dictate how long our safety might be assured. With your permission, I shall begin to calculate it.

QUEEN ELIZABETH. Yes yes yes, my dear Doctor. It's certain that one day mathematics will predict every facet of the world, but for moment I'm tired of hearing about it.

DOCTOR DEE. Thank you, my Queen. What a fine premonition!

BURBAGE. Oh, what an untimely wretched day!

QUEEN ELIZABETH. Master Burbage, the playhouse is no place for such drama!

BURBAGE. My queen. For my life, I cannot help it.

KEMP. Come now Burbage, think will you? Outside these doors could be some papist plot! So, you may tear your shirt with crying, but what's that to her?

(rhyming)

Our Fair Eliza hath rebellious wit

And scoffs aloud with those who mock her reign

By joining them she proves this simple bit

That she who laughs last laughs at those she's slain.

Thus treating treason like some savage jest

She raises up her axe against the rest

Until her Catholic victims do confess:

There's none can take a joke like Good Queen Bess.

*(**KEMP** mimes putting his head on the executioner's block and chopping it off. All are mortified, dreading the **QUEEN**'s response.)*

*(**QUEEN ELIZABETH** stares at **KEMP** for an interminably long time. Finally, she laughs.)*

QUEEN ELIZABETH. Master Shakespeare!

SHAKESPEARE. Your Majesty!

QUEEN ELIZABETH. You must write Kemp another comedy. Something with Falstaff in it.

BACON. An excellent idea, your Majesty.

QUEEN ELIZABETH. I know it is. I bloody well thought of it, didn't I?

BACON. As it happens, my Queen, I have commissioned a new play by Master Shakespeare – called *Falstaff in Love*, which I came to inspect.

KEMP. You've been holding out on us, Shakes!

QUEEN ELIZABETH. A new Falstaff play. My dear Master Shakespeare, you anticipate well.

DOCTOR DEE. An omen, my Queen! How the stars do align.

QUEEN ELIZABETH. Be quiet, John Dee! This news makes everyone pleased. Master Kemp, read it at once. Upstairs, perhaps.

BACON. I do hope you enjoy the commission, my Queen.

QUEEN ELIZABETH. Beware your pride, Master Bacon – it's not like you wrote it. Master Burbage, after some consideration I don't believe there's anything in this day that a good pot of ale wouldn't resolve. Do oblige me.

(*QUEEN ELIZABETH exits, followed by* **KEMP**, *the* **SOLDIERS** *and* **DOCTOR DEE.**)

SHAKESPEARE. Master Bacon –

BACON. If she likes it, I'll vouch for your play and you'll have your commission. Twenty pounds as we said.

SHAKESPEARE. Twenty?

BACON. In the meantime, do have a care with this carnage. We may be here awhile.

SHAKESPEARE. You expect me to clean this?

BACON. Well, it is your playhouse, after all.

SHAKESPEARE. It is also my play.

BACON. And I'm eager to hear what you've done with it.

(*BACON exits upstairs.*)

BURBAGE. A new Falstaff play?

SHAKESPEARE. Richard –

BURBAGE. I must bring her the ale.

(*BURBAGE exits.*)

(*The lights fade [LIGHT CUE 2].*)

ACT II

NIGHT

(Several hours later. The lights reveal a darker room [LIGHT CUE 3]. The bodies have been dragged away, and the tiring house floor is now mostly free from the carnage of earlier. **SHAKESPEARE** *sits alone.* **BURBAGE** *enters with a couple lit lanterns.)*

SHAKESPEARE. Richard, a moment please –

BURBAGE. It mortifies me Will, that you showed it to Francis Bacon first. We had an agreement.

*(***BURBAGE*** hangs the lanterns.)*

SHAKESPEARE. Well, now that – you have to understand that's not quite how it happened.

BURBAGE. You at least could have told me! Why would I want it after you've shown it around?

SHAKESPEARE. I don't know, Richard, the Queen demanded it. What does it matter? How was the reading?

BURBAGE. Oh, it's funny enough. Not quite up to your usual standards, but the bit with the basket is good. Did you really write it for Kemp?

SHAKESPEARE. Francis Bacon can be very persuasive.

BURBAGE. He is a crown lawyer.

SHAKESPEARE. But out of her favor. Why do you think he commissioned the play?

BURBAGE. To get in her favor? Do you think he'll succeed?

SHAKESPEARE. You heard the reading. Who cares either way if the play's any good, it still has my name.

BURBAGE. Should we produce it?

SHAKESPEARE. Not that we could, with half of our men now dead. Not to mention poor Kate.

BURBAGE. Don't.

SHAKESPEARE. Forgive me for that.

BURBAGE. I can still taste her kiss.

SHAKESPEARE. How bad do you think it is out there?

BURBAGE. I'm trying very hard not to think of it at all.

SHAKESPEARE. We've had plague before. In a month or two I'm sure this all shall blow over, and life will be back to normal.

BURBAGE. Have you stood on the roof? London Bridge has fallen and smoke hangs in the night too thick to breathe, but still there are flames from Moorgate to Fleet. There is nothing out there, except the affliction – and how far has it spread? Faster than Kemp's nine days to Norwich. Or perhaps even further.

SHAKESPEARE. No plague travels that fast.

BURBAGE. I think this is different.

(**RICE** *comes down the steps, still wearing that dress.*)

SHAKESPEARE. You're still in that dress.

RICE. I cannot reach the clasps.

BURBAGE. How goes it upstairs?

RICE. Bacon and Dee argue science while Kemp does a dance for the Queen.

SHAKESPEARE. You see? At least some things are normal.

BURBAGE. I think I speak truth when I say that this may be the worst day of my life.

RICE. At least it would make a great play.

SHAKESPEARE. No. It wouldn't.

RICE. No, but it would!

SHAKESPEARE. John – let me tell you a secret: Realistic drama is boring and dull. No audience would rather watch a single-room tragedy about our meager lives over a comic adventure where great men of history fight each other with wit and sword. Forgive me for saying, but this is simply not worth the effort.

RICE. What do you mean: not worth the effort?

SHAKESPEARE. Do you have any idea how difficult it is to run a company and also write plays? I can scarce find even a moment to sharpen a quill and set it to paper. Let alone scrounge up the coin to buy ink, paper, and candles. No, John. To say that an idea's worth my time is a bold statement indeed.

RICE. And bold statements are the very makings of drama. What better way to begin? Besides, it's certain to please, with death, monsters, and the Queen herself in a story that's true!

SHAKESPEARE. I'd be cautious of truth where the Queen is concerned. We are not some company of boys, who can conceal their bitter words with a sweet voice. There's no worse reproof than that of a patron who was grazed by your wit, so one must learn to be careful which ideas to pursue.

RICE. You speak from experience, sir?

SHAKESPEARE. Yes, but not mine. We can all thank Marlowe for his fine example.

(**SOLDIERS** *drag* **DOCTOR DEE** *in.* **BACON** *follows a few steps behind.*)

DOCTOR DEE. It is the cause, it is the cause! My soul!

BACON. The Queen has had enough of your tiresome discourse.

DOCTOR DEE. Master Bacon, I have observed things and learned things by a theory of numbers. The mathematics indicate a spread of affliction at a rate far beyond my initial assumption.

BACON. Ooo! Did the spirits tell you this?

DOCTOR DEE. No. I made this prediction through my calculations alone.

BACON. Calculations! Ha. Scientific predictions are made through observable truths, not conjured by numbers. Your methods aren't science, they're mere hocus pocus.

DOCTOR DEE. Maths are the model by which our universe works. You say it spreads through the bite, so if we travel by river the affliction won't reach us. If we can but retrieve the liquid meta-physic from my library in Mortlake –

BACON. No.

DOCTOR DEE. We can return here before dawn –

BACON. You will not leave this playhouse.

DOCTOR DEE. We cannot stay here.

BACON. I say we shall. The Queen is in danger, and until there's some evidence that we must take action, we'll keep our numbers right here. Master Kemp at this moment is painting the banner to signal for help. The Globe shall stay secure as long as its doors remain sealed. Any questions?

SHAKESPEARE. Did the Queen like the reading?

BACON. *What?* Oh, yes. A very good play, Master Shakespeare.

SHAKESPEARE. That's good. How was Kemp?

BACON. He spoke far more than was set down for him, and didn't speak the speech as I pronounced it to him, trippingly on the tongue, but mouthed it as if the town crier spoke the lines - sawing the air too much with his hand. I said suit the action to the word, the word to the action!

SHAKESPEARE. Did he do a jig?

BACON. Oh, it was villainous and showed a most pitiful ambition in the fool!

SHAKESPEARE. Yes, Kemp will do that.

DOCTOR DEE. Master Bacon, please, you must listen –

BACON. Doctor Dee, to continue this line is treason. Desist!

(**QUEEN ELIZABETH** *enters carrying the* Falstaff in Love *script. All bow.*)

QUEEN ELIZABETH. Oh, do get up.

DOCTOR DEE. Your Majesty, it was my understanding that the affliction –

QUEEN ELIZABETH. Doctor Dee, it was my understanding that you would be silent while Master Kemp did perform. But it would seem that even my understanding can be in error.

DOCTOR DEE. Forgive me, my Queen.

QUEEN ELIZABETH. Master Shakespeare. This Windsor play is one of your more middling creations.

BACON. Your Majesty, I –

QUEEN ELIZABETH. Francis Bacon, am I speaking to you? Tell me, Master Shakespeare, what has Jack Falstaff done to deserve such a treatment?

SHAKESPEARE. He died in my *Henry the Fifth,* your Majesty.

QUEEN ELIZABETH. His time in Hades has done him little good. He has returned from the dead a mere shadow of the knight we once knew. Indeed, your hand in this work is almost unrecognizable.

SHAKESPEARE. Forgive me, my Queen. The time between its commission and delivery was quite brief. I gave it little effort.

QUEEN ELIZABETH. That much is clear. Still, 'twill be a good role for Kemp. Once you revise it.

(**QUEEN ELIZABETH** *gives the script to* **SHAKESPEARE.**)

SHAKESPEARE. Yes. And perhaps I may better explain Falstaff's return.

QUEEN ELIZABETH. Or better yet, don't. Art needs no excuse if it is well-crafted.

BACON. Your Majesty –

QUEEN ELIZABETH. Now I am tired. Master Bacon, attend me. I have a sudden wish to hear your theory of science.

BACON. Your Majesty, I'll be delighted –

QUEEN ELIZABETH. As will I if it puts me to sleep.

(**QUEEN ELIZABETH** *exits, followed by* **BACON** *and the* **SOLDIERS.**)

DOCTOR DEE. I have calculated all, if they would but listen–

BURBAGE. What of this meta-physic you speak of, old man?

DOCTOR DEE. I shall explain. Of those elements which do comprise a man: blood, phlegm, and the biles black and yellow, each equate to the four elemental forces that shape our world – and thus are we each so composed in some part or another. And thereby to the rule of our humors are we subject, as one outweighs another, their flow within informs our disposition. And every physic may induce one humor – from blood to sanguine, black bile melanchol -

BURBAGE. Aye, yes. 'tis known. What of it?

DOCTOR DEE. It is this – now listen well. In those afflicted humors wax toward choler, with jaundiced angry thoughts. And so their flesh cries out for blood to balance the surfeit bile. This imbalance causeth great pain, and brings torment at every anguished step, so afflicted souls do shudder in their walk. But yet some melancholy must linger in their mind; to witness every sin their limbs commit. For while their gnashing teeth do rend the flesh how like the crocodi –

BURBAGE. Yes, yes. –

SHAKESPEARE. It is to be feared.

BURBAGE. More matter, less art.

DOCTOR DEE. I shall proceed. There is within my Mortlake home a firm-bound book embossed in hide which bears my sigil mark. Like so. Within this tome you'll find a formula deduced from the Roman Gallen's great alchemic works - a meta-physic which, when drunk, may stabilize man's humors. Of this draught there is, upon my shelf beside, one measured dram. If I could but go and fetch this drink.

SHAKESPEARE. Is it a cure?

DOCTOR DEE. Perhaps.

BURBAGE. Where is this house?

DOCTOR DEE. Upon the river, before the guild in Mortlake.

RICE. A white manor house?

DOCTOR DEE. Yes!

RICE. I know it.

BURBAGE. How?

RICE. I've passed it many times. By boat, at least.

DOCTOR DEE. The Queen's bark was shored not far from here, if we can but reach it –

RICE. I could get us there.

BURBAGE. You will not. When you were signed, I swore I would vouchsafe your care.

RICE. But sir!

DOCTOR DEE. He must! Or else we'll all die here!

BURBAGE. Be ware you'll fright the boy.

DOCTOR DEE. So let him fear! Each creeping day doth bring the reaper near. What is there in this life to fear but death? Our fate outside can be no worse than this. If we're not killed we'll starve.

BURBAGE. To leave the Globe is mad! 'Twill only with your corpse engorge their ranks! These dangers are too great for one so young.

DOCTOR DEE. The better he to learn what bravery is. You counterfeit a hero well onstage, why don't you play one now?

(**SOLDIER 1** *enters from upstairs. Tentative.*)

SOLDIER 1. Doctor?

DOCTOR DEE. Aye, lad. Come to do me some further disservice?

SOLDIER 1. No sir. Forgive the rough treatment. I bear you no malice, nor do I think the Globe as safe as Master Bacon insists. Indeed, even if we should last the night, there's no guarantee what tomorrow will bring. If those creatures are true to what I've seen, I cannot imagine much remains beyond these walls.

SHAKESPEARE. What did you see?

SOLDIER 1. I was recruiting in Cheapside when the affliction broke out. Only this morning. God, it feels like ages. We were told it was a brawl near Temple Gate. At first I thought it nothing but maybe some Catholic unrest – but by the time we arrived it was no brawl, just... madness. The way they moved, and in their eyes this – rage. We were soon outnumbered, and then even moreso as those that fell did rise again, afflicted. I don't know how I managed, but I ran. There was all around me a great press of people crossing the Thames. A great horde of men and women all fleeing the City, with carts, horses, loaded down with everything they owned. No sooner did I cross the bridge into Southwark, than the cry of affliction rose behind me. In a panic, the guards dropped the gates. You could see those poor fools on the bridge – climbing, crushing each other, pressing hands of money through the bars – until that inhuman fury clouded their eyes. We had to contain it. So they bombarded the bridge. And it fell. I then found myself in Lord Cecil's service, which in turn led me here.

SHAKESPEARE. Do you mean to stay here?

SOLDIER 1. There's nothing left for any of us. To leave or to stay, what difference is that? You're going, aren't you?

RICE. We are.

BURBAGE. Not you, John.

SHAKESPEARE. Is there anyone else who can pilot a bark?

RICE. Then I shall go.

SOLDIER 1. How can I help you in this?

SHAKESPEARE. You, lad, must stay with the Queen. Seal the door when we've gone and await Lord Cecil's signal.

SOLDIER 1. Thrice and thrice, I recall.

SHAKESPEARE. Good. Doctor Dee, Burbage and I shall defend the way till we reach the Queen's boat.

DOCTOR DEE. If we are quick enough, the tides will be in our favor. We can travel to Mortlake unseen and return here by dawn. To travel by day would be deadly for sure. Are we ready?

RICE. Yes, sir.

SHAKESPEARE. 'tis better than to stay here.

BURBAGE. Will, this is folly.

SHAKESPEARE. Richard, what choice do we have?

BURBAGE. Are you taking that script?

SHAKESPEARE. It is my play, is it not?

DOCTOR DEE. You'll close us out?

SOLDIER 1. Knock thrice and thrice on your return.

DOCTOR DEE. Be quick when we do. Thus ready? We go.

(**DEE** *opens the door.* **BACON** *and* **SOLDIER 2** *come down the stair. All turn to face them.*)

BACON. What business is this? Shut the door!

SOLDIER 1. Go, bring this elixir.

BACON. I say shut the door!

SHAKESPEARE. Sir, vouchsafe the Queen. We will return by dawn.

BACON. You won't leave with that script.

(**BACON** *draws his sword and begins to advance.* **SOLDIER 2** *follows suit.*)

SHAKESPEARE. It's mine, is it not?

(**SHAKESPEARE** *draws his sword.* **BURBAGE** *and* **SOLDIER 1** *follow suit.*)

DOCTOR DEE. Come! Your noise will draw the afflicted unless we go now!

RICE. Sir, I go!

(**RICE** *runs out the door.*)

DOCTOR DEE. Burbage!

BURBAGE. I feel weak.

DOCTOR DEE. Then I must.

(**DOCTOR DEE** *turns to exit, but discovers an afflicted* **KATE** *standing there.*)

DOCTOR DEE. God mark me!

(**DEE** *stands aside.* **BURBAGE** *sees her.*)

BURBAGE. Kate! She's returned!

(With a vicious shriek, the Afflicted **KATE** *bursts into the room and attacks the unsuspecting* **SOLDIER 1**, *sinking her teeth into him. He falls to his knees.)*

SOLDIER 1. Oh God help me!

BURBAGE. Kate!

*(***KATE*** *reels back and stares at* **BURBAGE**, *her mouth now dripping with blood.)*

SHAKESPEARE. Oh, that's not good.

*(***KATE*** *charges* **BURBAGE**. **SHAKESPEARE** *cuts* **KATE** — *her hands clawing out as she collapses and dies.)*

SHAKESPEARE. I'm sorry, dear Kate.

SOLDIER 1. *(moaning softly)* God help me. God help me.

BACON. I said close the door.

SHAKESPEARE. And I say we shall not!

BACON. Then I shall close it for thee!

*(***BACON*** *lunges at* **SHAKESPEARE**. **SHAKESPEARE** *parries.* **BACON** *and* **SHAKESPEARE** *fight.)*

SHAKESPEARE. Go Doctor Dee. Get you gone, Richard!

DOCTOR DEE. Master Shakespeare, they come!

*(***BACON*** *pins* **SHAKESPEARE**. **SHAKESPEARE** *hits* **BACON** *with his script.)*

SHAKESPEARE. Go, Richard! Find the boy!

*(***BACON*** *tries to close the door, but* **SHAKESPEARE** *prevents him. They continue to fight.)*

BURBAGE. Will, do not do this!

SOLDIER 2. Put up your sword!

*(***QUEEN ELIZABETH*** *and* **KEMP** *come down the stairs. Outside the door, the afflicted are starting to approach, drawn by the sound of the fight.)*

QUEEN ELIZABETH. What racket is this!

BACON. Treason, my queen!

KEMP. Oh, well done now, Shakes!

BACON. Be still, Master Kemp! Dee –

DOCTOR DEE. I cannot! I cannot! They come.

> (**BURBAGE** *threatens* **SHAKESPEARE** *with his sword, surprising him.*)

BURBAGE. Dee, close the door. Thy sword, Will.

> (**SHAKESPEARE** *gives* **BURBAGE** *his sword.* **DOCTOR DEE** *closes the door.*)

DOCTOR DEE. Forgive me my Queen.

SOLDIER 1. *(moaning softly)* ...God help me. Oh please.

> (*The afflicted claw upon the door.*)

BACON. Put out the candles and quiet that man. Master Shakespeare, my script.

SHAKESPEARE. It must have revisions.

BACON. Give o'er the play.

> (**BACON** *takes the script.*)

BACON. Lights! Lights! Lights!

> (**KEMP** *and* **DOCTOR DEE** *put out the lanterns, darkening the room [LIGHT CUE 4].* **SOLDIER 2** *kills* **SOLDIER 1.**)

KEMP. Put out the light, and then put out the light.

QUEEN ELIZABETH. It is my great desire to know precisely what hath here occurred.

BACON. These men and that boy conspired to break from this Globe, and exposed us thereby to the threat of affliction!

DOCTOR DEE. Think you these wooden planks and walls of loam will long withstand the ravaging hordes, whose cankerous bite turns all men to beast? The igneous plague shall blow through these streets until all life is thereby consumed! How may we withstand it?

BACON. Still you breathe foul sedition to the very soul. By sending this boy to the streets, you have as much committed murder as treason, for from this insurrectious breach he shall be as like to die as we.

KEMP. Aye Master Bacon, give but a word, and I'll grab him by the philosopher's stones and bring him to reason!

QUEEN ELIZABETH. Master Shakespeare, is it true what is said?

SHAKESPEARE. Your majesty, it is.

QUEEN ELIZABETH. I am eager to hear it.

SHAKESPEARE. My queen, I haven't the words.

QUEEN ELIZABETH. Then you must simply invent them.

(**QUEEN ELIZABETH** *exits upstairs.*)

BACON. Escort them upstairs.

(**SOLDIER 2** *escorts* **SHAKESPEARE** *and* **DOCTOR DEE** *upstairs.*)

BACON. Master Kemp, how's the banner?

KEMP. Beautiful. It says "Help! Queen within."

BACON. Raise it at dawn.

(**KEMP** *follows the rest.* **BURBAGE** *looks stricken.*)

BACON. What, Master Burbage, no soliloquy?

BURBAGE. Sir, I am wretched.

BACON. So you are. Are you sure you're unbitten? Come Master Burbage, your sword has earned a reprieve for your part in this treason. Do join us upstairs when you're settled – Master Shakespeare's telling of young Rice's escape shall be a tale that none wish to miss.

(**BACON** *exits.*)

(*Lights fade [LIGHT CUE 5].*)

ACT III

DAWN

(The lights come up to reveal the tiring house in darkness [LIGHT CUE 6]. No candles, just moonlight and distant flames.)

(The bodies have been cleared. **SHAKESPEARE** *and* **DOCTOR DEE** *sit with hands manacled.* **DEE** *is asleep. Nearby* **SOLDIER 2** *watches over them, but even he is nodding off.)*

*(***BURBAGE*** *approaches.* **SOLDIER 2** *stands.)*

SOLDIER 2. Who's there?

BURBAGE. Long live the Queen.

SOLDIER 2. Burbage?

BURBAGE. He. Tis almost dawn, friend, get thee to bed. I will stand for thee.

SOLDIER 2. For this relief much thanks.

*(***SOLDIER 2*** *goes upstairs.* **BURBAGE** *checks the door.)*

SHAKESPEARE. Hallo, Richard. Now this is familiar, I'm clapped in irons whilst you play the villain.

BURBAGE. Don't be unfair.

SHAKESPEARE. Too right. This time you don't speak my words, the villainy is thine own.

BURBAGE. Will, this isn't a play.

SHAKESPEARE. All the world's a stage, isn't that what we say?

BURBAGE. Please don't be glib, I saved your life.

SHAKESPEARE. How does this save me?

BURBAGE. From dueling Francis Bacon? Or leaving the Globe? You're mad to imagine that either would have ended better than this.

SHAKESPEARE. We're doomed either way, Richard, why not take a chance? You were ready to join us, but then forced us to stay!

BURBAGE. God, Will! May a man not want two things?

SHAKESPEARE. Like Kate and your wife?

BURBAGE. Or a life in London and a family in Stratford! We're all of two minds, Will. There's no harm in that. (beat) Unless there is. Oh that would be a tragedy to write! A great melancholy hero, torn by indecision between vengeance and death. To take up arms or to take my own life? Something like that. To be or... not be? You'd write it better, I'd just act it well.

SHAKESPEARE. It would be perfect for you. Should I give it some scenes where the dead walk again?

BURBAGE. You needn't be vicious.

SHAKESPEARE. I'm sorry. How are you?

BURBAGE. Everything aches, and I cannot sleep.

SHAKESPEARE. Nay, nor can I. What do you think has become of young John?

BURBAGE. He'll fare no worse than Kate.

SHAKESPEARE. No. Oh, how do I say this – Richard, um, you must know that Kate and I, after my son, for a time we …

BURBAGE. Oh, Will, please don't. I know.

SHAKESPEARE. You do?

BURBAGE. She read me your sonnets. They're really quite good.

SHAKESPEARE. She said not to tell you. Do you know how long I've suffered with this?

BURBAGE. Then why root it up if it grieves you so much? Will, please – what's past is past.

SHAKESPEARE. If it were only that simple. You haven't endured the death of a child.

BURBAGE. We don't know that, now do we?

SHAKESPEARE. No.

BURBAGE. You know, we should have remounted your Richard the Third. Such a good role.

SHAKESPEARE. I'm glad that we didn't. Some plays once they're done should simply stay dead.

BURBAGE. Oh, audience loved that one.

SHAKESPEARE. As I recall, the audience loved your Richard, whilst I as your Clarence waited in gaol for the death your ambition would inevitably bring. Tell me does art imitate life, or is it the other way 'round?

BURBAGE. You can't blame me for this. Besides, we all have ambitions. There's even one Clarence that fell in your wake.

SHAKESPEARE. Don't say you mean Kemp. You know, Richard, I think for the moment I am tired of history.

BURBAGE. What wonder is that? Under your pen, I've played the full line of Lancaster and a good share of York. Continue this trend and I'd have played the Old Boot before the year's end.

SHAKESPEARE. You'd play her so well.

BURBAGE. Well, I'd make it my own. *(mimicking the* **QUEEN***)* "Do as I want and not as I say. The whim of Eliza's the law of the day!" Could you write a play for her?

SHAKESPEARE. Have I not already done that?

BURBAGE. I meant a good play, not one demanded by Bacon.

SHAKESPEARE. It could be both, if he would but let me. You wish to speak of ambition? One with his look would murder a Clarence with hardly a wink.

BURBAGE. Oh come now, Bacon isn't awful – till your logic be at fault. So, tell me, how much did he dictate of *Falstaff in Love?*

SHAKESPEARE. More than his share.

BURBAGE. Didn't write it, did you?

SHAKESPEARE. I never said that.

BURBAGE. Oh bollocks, Will. You didn't have to. A new play for Kemp? It's apparent enough.

SHAKESPEARE. True. Why pen yet another script for him to wipe his jigging arse with?

BURBAGE. Don't be crass, Will. We were lucky to have him. We'd have long since folded without that homespun coxcomb with his dog on a string. Recall how they came by the thousand to see his pranks? Tactless really. Funny, but tactless. Hardly matters now.

SHAKESPEARE. It matters to me.

BURBAGE. So your verses were trampled. When he'd burst into jest in the midst of the scene, it may have been coarse, but by God it was fun. Things always strung together well enough.

SHAKESPEARE. You see? That's just it! My plays aren't just strung together like flowers on a garland, they're constructed – like this playhouse.

BURBAGE. How do you mean?

SHAKESPEARE. Only that they're stolen piece by piece.

BURBAGE. I didn't steal this playhouse!

SHAKESPEARE. Oh Burbage, please. Save it for Bacon. We both know every plank, board and tile was stolen from Shoreditch and rebuilt in Southwark to suit our needs. So it is for me not with lumber, but with thoughts, words, and deeds.

BURBAGE. I suppose you may borrow a story from time to time.

SHAKESPEARE. Yes, but always with an oath to give it back when I'm done! Burbage, I steal them - from words on the street to thoughts in a book. Every waking moment of life is rendered up to make my art. As a joiner cuts lumber to form, so from this daily accumulation do I craft my plays. And if I should be commissioned to use an idea with no merit, well then I employ the suggestion in some decorative way, such that the one who supplied it, seeing it so used, thinks well of me, little realizing that the most important components are often deepest buried. Like a solid foundation.

(**BURBAGE** *has fallen asleep.*)

SHAKESPEARE. What silent now, Richard? Aye, 'tis late enough. Rest well, good friend. Would I could join you.

(*The sound of* KEMP *arriving.*)

SHAKESPEARE. Hallo, Master Kemp. I hear your bells.

KEMP. I heard voices. Not unguarded are you?

SHAKESPEARE. Oh no, Burbage stands watch.

KEMP. Sits it, you mean. Good thing he does, so any misconduct is not on my head. What think you, dear Shakes, to share this sad sack? You won't likely find more.

SHAKESPEARE. Ah, what the hey. I could do with a sip. Will you now bend my ear for a new play as well?

KEMP. Some good that would be, I won't get to play it.

SHAKESPEARE. You at least had the reading. How did it go? Did her majesty laugh?

KEMP. You may not like what I do, but the Queen's always enjoyed my roles.

SHAKESPEARE. Firstly - I wrote them. So they're my roles, not yours. And second, the Queen's not a playwright – so I might know a bit more about it than she.

KEMP. Yet when she asks for a new Falstaff play, lo! – there it is. So you see why her opinion matters a bit more than yours.

SHAKESPEARE. It's still my pen that writes them, though, isn't it?

KEMP. Is it now?

(SHAKESPEARE *doesn't answer.*)

KEMP. Oh-ho-ho, I knew it! Don't you dare protest, dear Will, for I know your pen and Kemp drinks with no liars!

SHAKESPEARE. Alright, Kemp. Touché. Now pass.

KEMP. Well, I'd say you've earned it. Hey, do you know what I see as the issue you face?

SHAKESPEARE. I cannot sleep?

KEMP. You're a-feared.

SHAKESPEARE. A-feared? In a burning city filled with afflicted, each friend of mine dead except dear snoring Richard, and my wife and two children unknowing in Stratford, of course I'm a-feared. So please Master Kemp, I'm eager to hear, what makes this my issue? Ye gods, do you never get a-feared?

KEMP. Not like you dear Will, you're a-feared of success.

SHAKESPEARE. Not much chance of that now, is there? Why ever do I tell you anything?

KEMP. Because you trust me.

SHAKESPEARE. Do I?

KEMP. Well I think you do, even if you don't.

SHAKESPEARE. How's that then?

KEMP. We're eye-to-eye, you and I. We've known each other what, some ten summers? Sure we've our differences, but never a lie passed between us - and that's something, isn't it? So you want to write good plays. I want to play good roles. We had our successes though, didn't we? - I mean Dogberry was good, and Bottom, you liked that. And Falstaff.

SHAKESPEARE. Oh Falstaff. He was – oh he could have been so much more.

KEMP. Ah, he just meant different things to us. The audience loved him either way, so who are we to begrudge that of him, or them, or each other? You are too somber. Even you must admit it was a good life. Here. To the end of hard feelings.

SHAKESPEARE. To the end of all feelings.

KEMP. Don't be morose! At least when you die you'll still have your plays. What's left of me?

SHAKESPEARE. My plays are just for the amusement of friends, not fit for the ages. The only words that survive me will be writ on my stone. And now perhaps not even that.

KEMP. And what would those be?

SHAKESPEARE. "Good friends for Jesus sake forbeare,
    To dig the dust enclosed here.
    Blessed be the man that spares these stones,
    And cursed be he that moves my bones."

(**KEMP** *laughs.* **SHAKESPEARE** *smiles.*)

KEMP. He lives! Beware that smile, dear Will, your armor is cracking. Or is this the end of somber Shakespeare? So when'd you polish that little gem?

SHAKESPEARE. One never knows when a good epitaph might be of use.

KEMP. Well, much as it suits you, and I assure you it does, such posthumous posturing is not for me. Let my grave simply say "Kemp, a man."

SHAKESPEARE. "A man." Is that all?

KEMP. 'Tis true, is it not? Or is it too much? Well then, perhaps simply "Kemp."

SHAKESPEARE. It's hardly enough for a fellow of infinite jest. What of your gibes? your gambols? your songs? your flashes of merriment, that are wont to set the table on a roar?

KEMP. Why, they'll be in my grave with me.

SHAKESPEARE. Then 'twill be a sad place indeed.

KEMP. Not with my jests in there! I shall amuse myself till judgment day!

SHAKESPEARE. That may not be long hence now.

KEMP. No, I'd imagine it's not. Dawn is approaching. I should put up the banner. Bacon asked me to fly it, but I'm not sure for whom. When I look past the river, I see only flames. But alas, alas, alack-a-day hey nonny, hey nonny, nonny hey!

(**KEMP** *dances his way upstairs.*)

DOCTOR DEE. He's wiser than most.

SHAKESPEARE. How did you hear that? Were you not asleep?

DOCTOR DEE. In college one learns to both listen and sleep. Fools often speak truth.

SHAKESPEARE. Be careful what you say of Kemp, that could go to his head.

DOCTOR DEE. Let it go to thine instead. Yea, every man seeking truth needs a fool now and then, whose unschooled and untutored self can see through the veil that learning obscures. Where age and knowledge clouds men's eyes, the fool can see unfettered by his wit and from his mouth issues forth God's truth. So my scrying Edmund and your Master Kemp have each made our names.

SHAKESPEARE. Well, that may be so, but I don't have to like it.

DOCTOR DEE. I know I never have. But so it is. You know, I once penned a play myself, back in my Cambridge days. Oh it was marvelous, with an immense flying scarab. In fact, since I started at Manchester, I've been at work on a new play.

SHAKESPEARE. Oh?

DOCTOR DEE. A wronged magician, isolated on a remote island, summons through the spirits the very man who was his oppressor at court. I've been hoping to find a collaborator!

SHAKESPEARE. Yes, well -

DOCTOR DEE. It's quite apropos. Very timely, I think. I call it, *The Hurricano*. Will you undertake it?

SHAKESPEARE. Alack, sir, I if only I could, but now my poems are all o'erthrown.

(*BACON comes down the steps, followed by* **SOLDIER 2**.)

BACON. And they sit here unguarded.

SOLDIER 2. He gave me reprieve.

BACON. And now look at him.

SHAKESPEARE. Let him sleep. He is unwell, and we're all tired enough.

BACON. The Queen may sleep, but we cannot. There's much work to be done.

SHAKESPEARE. Like waiting and waiting.

BACON. We can still signal for help.

SHAKESPEARE. From whom? I've heard no church bells chime, not even the cock crows today.

DOCTOR DEE. Master Bacon, again I insist, we should leave the Globe at once. If we can reach the river by daybreak and thence make it to Mortlake, we may yet save our England.

BACON. Tell me what there is to save? Beyond these walls it may be that no England remains. No nation is ought but the labor of men, and outside this wooden O we'll find none of that. Only smoke and shadow.

DOCTOR DEE. I assure you, if we can but make it to Mortlake, I can devise a cure for the affliction - what a fine metaphysic that would be!

BACON. Doctor Dee, I hereby ban your use of the word 'metaphysic'.

DOCTOR DEE. Ah, no!

BACON. Then you must at least not misuse it. Metaphysics are those formal and final causes from which all physical truths derive. Is there not in all our great language some better phrase you could use for such unscientific and inconsistent ideas as alchemy and spirits?

SHAKESPEARE. Master Bacon, language holds a mirror to our nature. You cannot dictate its use. As men's fortunes must change, so shall our words. All men to strive towards improvement. Is our language any different?

BACON. And what improvement may be had by those clawing this door? Is there any mastery they can achieve?

SHAKESPEARE. I see you take a dim view on the betterment of man.

BACON. You're one to speak. "First thing we'll do is kill all the lawyers" did you not say that?

SHAKESPEARE. A character did. In a play that I wrote. No wonder you think me a regicide too, for at least two dozen monarchs have died by this hand. Here's my advice: don't try to find me in words that I pen. My plays aren't prayers, essays, or private thoughts, but merely words words words and some inkblots.

(**KEMP** *comes running downstairs.*)

KEMP. I don't mean to frighten, but the blaze crossed the river, perhaps on the wind. From the roof I spied fierce flames approaching, with a smoke so dark that it blots out the stars!

BACON. How far?

KEMP. Mere buildings away. One gust could consume us.

BACON. Then we must leave at once.

SOLDIER 2. What about the banner?

KEMP. It won't stave off the flames.

DOCTOR DEE. Had we but left when I said that we should, we would now be safely in Mortlake!

BACON. Shut up, old man!

SHAKESPEARE. If we go on the street, we must all be armed.

SOLDIER 2. So you can renew prior treasons?

SHAKESPEARE. So I can fight for my life.

DOCTOR DEE. To be on the streets with shackled hands would be doom.

BACON. Alright. You'll have your hands, but no weapons. (*to* **SOLDIER 2**) Go wake the Queen.

SOLDIER 2. Sir, I shall.

(**BACON** *undoes* **DOCTOR DEE**'s *shackles with a key.* **SOLDIER 2** *goes toward the stairs. Now freed,* **DOCTOR DEE** *attempts to wake* **BURBAGE**.)

DOCTOR DEE. Master Burbage, arise.

SHAKESPEARE. Burbage, get up.

(**BACON** *starts to unlock* **SHAKESPEARE**'s *shackles. Suddenly, an afflicted* **BURBAGE** *awakens and bites* **DOCTOR DEE**.)

DOCTOR DEE. Oh ye angels and ministers of grace, defend us!

(**SOLDIER 2** *returns to attack* **BURBAGE**. **BURBAGE** *and* **SOLDIER 2** *fight.* **DOCTOR DEE** *rushes to unbar the door.*)

BACON. Do not open the door! Stop him!

(BACON runs to stop DOCTOR DEE, taking the key.)

SHAKESPEARE. What of my chains!?

SOLDIER 2. Oh God! Oh God!

KEMP. Will, get down.

(KEMP overturns a table and pulls SHAKESPEARE under it, hiding them. KEMP begins undoing his bells.)

(The Afflicted BURBAGE kills SOLDIER 2, and then charges BACON.)

(DOCTOR DEE unbars the door. It flies open and several AFFLICTED burst in, attacking him.)

DOCTOR DEE. Aaugh.

(DOCTOR DEE is bitten and killed. BACON draws his sword to fight BURBAGE, but is bitten before he can attack.)

(KEMP races forward, bells in hand.)

SHAKESPEARE. Kemp, what are you doing!?

(KEMP runs up to BURBAGE and jangles the bells at him. BURBAGE releases BACON.)

(All afflicted stare in amazement as KEMP waves his bells. KEMP throws his bells out the door. The AFFLICTED follow the sound out.)

(KEMP grabs the severely wounded BACON and drags him behind the overturned table.)

KEMP. The key.

(BACON sets down his sword and undoes SHAKESPEARE's manacles. BACON is badly wounded.)

SHAKESPEARE. You don't look good, sir.

BACON. I've seen better days. You must save the Queen.

KEMP. That's easier said.

(The afflicted are beginning to return to the playhouse.)

BACON. Master Shakespeare, go upstairs. Kemp, give me your bells. You must hold the entrance till I've lured them out onto the street.

SHAKESPEARE. Master Bacon, you're sure?

BACON. I've nothing to lose, now have I? Here, Master Shakespeare –

(*BACON gives his script to* **SHAKESPEARE.**)

SHAKESPEARE. Your script?

BACON. Yours, mine, it's no matter who wrote it as long as the words live on. Promise me?

SHAKESPEARE. Of course.

BACON. My thanks. When I leave the Globe, do shut me out.

KEMP. Sir.

(*KEMP give his bells to* **BACON**. **BACON** *picks up his sword, then stands up and jangles the bells. The afflicted all turn to watch him, mesmerized.*)

BACON. Go now!

(**SHAKESPEARE** *runs toward the stairs, but as he approaches, an Afflicted* **SOLDIER 2** *rises, blocking his path, and knocking him down.*)

SHAKESPEARE. Ahhh!

BACON. Here!

(**BACON**, *now surrounded by afflicted, kicks his sword to* **SHAKESPEARE**. **SHAKESPEARE** *grabs the sword and fights the Afflicted* **SOLDIER 2**.)

(*But the moment of distraction was too much.* **BACON** *is no longer ringing the bells. The afflicted emerge from their torpor and attack him.*)

BACON. Auugh!

(**BACON** *is dragged down, bitten, and killed.* **SHAKESPEARE** *throws off* **SOLDIER 2** *as* **KEMP** *races forward to grab the bells.*)

KEMP. No!

SHAKESPEARE. Kemp!

(**KEMP** *jingles the bells, dancing through the swarming afflicted.*)

SHAKESPEARE. Kemp!

KEMP. Don't fret, dear Shakerags. I have bells enough for this!

SHAKESPEARE. What are you doing?

KEMP. Just a little laughing jig. Don't worry, I'll be Norwich soon enough.

SHAKESPEARE. You can't be serious.

KEMP. When have I ever been serious? Now be a friend, William, shut the door when I go.

SHAKESPEARE. Yes, Kemp. Thank you. Godspeed, old friend.

KEMP. Come friends, come friends and see the Nine Days Wonder in me!

(**KEMP** *jigs out the door with his bells. A pied piper leading the afflicted away from the playhouse.*)

(**SHAKESPEARE** *moves towards the door.*)

SHAKESPEARE. Thus civil blood makes civil hands unclean, and the cry is still 'They come'.

(*The horde of* **AFFLICTED** *departs, revealing* **JOHN RICE** *in the doorway, his dress now ragged and torn. He carries a small vial in his hand. He moves with great difficulty, as though each breath causes him pain.*)

RICE. I wonder - how many goodly creatures are there here?

SHAKESPEARE. John!

(**RICE** *staggers in.* **SHAKESPEARE** *closes the door.*)

RICE. Oh, Master Shakespeare, how hideous mankind is. O grave new world that hath such people in't. Here is the Doctor's vial. But no medicine in the world can do me good; the dread affliction now works its course. What's here befallen?

SHAKESPEARE. The sight is dismal, and thy affairs from Mortlake come too late.

RICE. Nay, come not near me. Here's the smell of blood still. Shakespeare, I am dead. The potent poison quite o'er-crows my spirit. Yet I must die, else I'll betray more men. Is this a dagger I see before me?

SHAKESPEARE. My sword, dear lad.

RICE. I prithee, Shakespeare, stay thou by me. Thou art a fellow of a good respect, thy life hath had some smatch of honour in it. Hold then thy sword, and turn away thy face, while I do run upon it. Wilt thou, Shakespeare?

SHAKESPEARE. Give me your hand first.

(**SHAKESPEARE** *offers* **RICE** *his hand. A pounding is heard on the door. It continues intermittently.*)

RICE. All the perfumes of Arabia will not sweeten this hand. Oh, oh, oh!

SHAKESPEARE. There's a knocking at the gate. Come, come, come, come, give me your hand. Fare you well, my boy.

RICE. Farewell, good Shakespeare.

(**RICE** *throws himself upon Shakespeare's sword.* **RICE** *collapses.* **SHAKESPEARE** *drops the sword and catches* **RICE** *in his arms, lowering him to the floor.*)

RICE. What's done cannot be undone. A guiltless death I die. I pray you, sir, undo this button.

SHAKESPEARE. Fear not, dear John. Though thou may be dressed a maid, thou wilt die a player.

RICE. I thank you, sir. The rest is silence.

(**RICE** *dies.*)

(*The door bursts open.* **AFFLICTED** *slowly fill room and those who died earlier now rise. But none notice the seated* **SHAKESPEARE.**)

SHAKESPEARE. Good night, sweet apprentice. And flights of angels sing thee to thy rest. I hop'd thou shouldst have been my Hamlet's wife; and a thousand other roles I might have made for thee, poor player, that scarce did strut or fret thy hour on the stage and now is heard no more. Out, out brief candle – so it is with walking shadows

Fate doth end our tale as all tales must -

Where once was mirth, there now is dust.

When foul Affliction makes this truth quite plain

In Shakespeare's land only the dead shall reign.

(An afflicted **QUEEN ELIZABETH** *descends the stairs.)*

(Sensing the presence of **SHAKESPEARE** *all other afflicted crouch as if ready to pounce, or almost as if they bow to their* **QUEEN** *[LIGHT CUE 7].)*

END OF PLAY

(Followed by an Elizabethan curtain call dance [LIGHT CUE 8, SOUND CUE 4].)

APPENDIX A: Production Notes

ON AFFLICTION

Elizabethans used the term "affliction" to mean madness, illness, or demonic possession – and wouldn't have known how to distinguish these maladies. The Affliction of this play represents a combination of these ideas.

Affliction is spread by saliva, such as a bite or a kiss. There are no specific rules for killing the Afflicted, but even when killed, they will rise again after a certain amount of time.

The Afflicted have two distinct states: torpor and frenzy. Torpor is a state of shambling distraction. Frenzy is a state of violent bloodlust. Regardless of their state, the Afflicted should always represent a legitimate threat.

ON THE QUOTES

There are two types of Shakespearean references in this play. The first type of reference is contextual: when someone mentions something written prior to 1599. When characters speak about these works it is always with an awareness of the source.

The second type of reference is meta-theatrical: the various quotes and misquotes that pepper the text. There are all drawn from Shakespeare's plays written after 1599. The characters should deliver these lines as though they are being spoken for the first time.

ON BLOOD AND GORE

These effects can be fun, but are not strictly necessary. If used, they should not impede the action of the play.

APPENDIX B: Supplementary Performance Text

The following texts may be delivered 'onstage' during Act 1:

HENRY V, ACT 5

The following casting should be obeyed:

SHAKESPEARE as Burgundy/Chorus

BURBAGE as Henry V

RICE as Princess Katharine

SINKLO as the King of France

KEMP'S NINE DAYS WONDER SPEECH

Delivered by **KEMP** from the playhouse stage, to both applause and music.

KEMP.

> Honorable friends and well-wishers all!
> I, Master Kemp, your beloved cavaliero -
> maker of jigs and all method of merriment,
> recently of these Lord Chamberlain's men -
> Am here to announce to your great acclaim
> The work of an age: Kemp's Nine Days Wonder.
> What's that you say, what wonders are these?
> Performed in a Morris from London to Norwich
> with all the pleasure, pains and kind entertainment
> one might expect between here and there!
> Hark, again, I hear you cry: What care should I have?
> There are some of this stage who do me decry
> with envious words and slanderous lie
> But with this fine dance, I shall them reprove
> nothing hurtful, just merriment's what I pursue
> So gentles and rough folk, I repeat my refrain
> Come see how I'm welcomed, and by whom entertained
> At the first of my days, the Lord Mayor sets my pace
> But with your kind hands, I shall offer a taste!
> So, come friends, come friends,
> on the first Lenten Monday,
> and see the Nine Days Wonder in me!

SOUND AND LIGHT CUE LIST

ACT 1

    LIGHT 1 – lights up on Act 1 (evening)

    SOUND 1 – Explosion of bridge outside

    SOUND 2 – Cheers, applause, stamping from the stage

    SOUND 3 – Laughter and cheering from the stage

    LIGHT 2 – lights out (end of act)

ACT 2

    LIGHT 3 – lights up on Act 2 (night)

    LIGHT 4 – the room darkens as the lanterns are extinguished

    LIGHT 5 – lights out (end of act)

ACT 3

    LIGHT 6 – lights up on Act 3 (early dawn)

    LIGHT 7 – lights out (end of play)

    LIGHT 8 – lights up for curtain call

    SOUND 4 – curtain call dance

PROP LIST

PRESET ONSTAGE

table
2 chairs
bench
2 barrels
2 chests
2 buckets
basket
prop swords (in the barrels)
the players' change of clothes (in the baskets)
a lute (on the bench)
a canvas wig head (on the table)
a long wooden bar (near the door)

ACT 1

Morris bells (**KEMP**)
wicker basket (**KATE**)
tearable shirts (in **KATE**'s basket)
Princess Katharine wig (**RICE**)
sword (on **BACON**)
"Falstaff in Love" script (**BACON**)
swords (the **SOLDIERS**)
sword (**CECIL**)
bandage (**CECIL**)
journal and pencil (**DEE**)

ACT 2

2 lanterns (**BURBAGE**)

ACT 3

2 sets of manacles (**SHAKESPEARE**, **DEE**)
jug of wine (**KEMP**)
key (**BACON**)
vial of elixir (**RICE**)

COSTUME LIST

WILLIAM SHAKESPEARE
Henry 5 costume; Elizabethan street clothes

RICHARD BURBAGE
Henry 5 costume; Elizabethan street clothes

WILL KEMP
Elizabethan street clothes (with Morris bells)

JOHN RICE
Henry 5 dress; distressed version

KATE BRAITHWAITE
Washerwoman clothes; distressed/afflicted version

JOHN SINKLO
Henry 5 costume; Elizabethan street clothes; distressed/afflicted version

FRANCIS BACON
Expensive clothes (with sword)

SIR ROBERT CECIL
Expensive clothes (with sword); distressed/afflicted version

QUEEN ELIZABETH TUDOR
Royal finery and crown

DOCTOR JOHN DEE
Academic robes and skullcap

SOLDIER 1
Uniform (with sword)

SOLDIER 2
Uniform (with sword)

OTHER PLAYERS
Henry 5 costume; Elizabethan street clothes; distressed/afflicted version

OTHER SOLDIERS
Soldier uniform (with sword); distressed/afflicted version

AFFLICTED
Distressed Elizabethan clothes

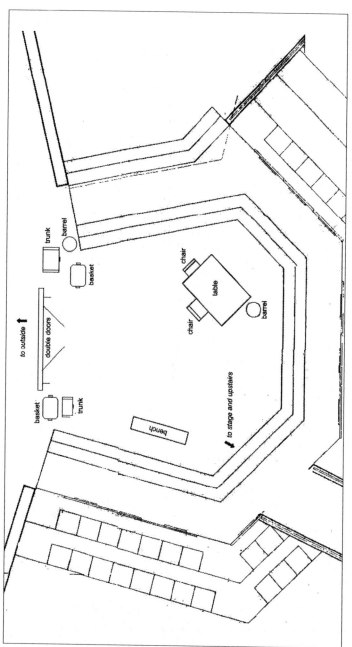

Set design by David Pisa

OTHER TITLES AVAILABLE FROM SAMUEL FRENCH

THE PEOPLE VS. FRIAR LAURENCE: THE MAN WHO KILLED ROMEO AND JULIET

Ron West and Phil Swann

Musical Comedy / 6m, 3f / Simple set

A musical comedy spoof starring the Friar of Shakespeare's Romeo and Juliet! Friar Laurence is behind bars, charged for the 'murder' of the lovers. As the trial progresses, mayhem and silliness abound with bits, songs, and scenes equal parts Vaudeville and Bard. A "load of laughs" (*Chicago Sun Times*, highly recommended), *The People Vs. Friar Laurence: The Man who Killed Romeo and Juliet* is sure to leave both Shakespeare scholars and low-brow humorists rolling in the aisles!

"Hysterical—West and Swann have shrouded the tale with witty story devices and a bright cloak of catchy songs that add to the ribald humor while moving the story along in the best traditions of musical theatre."
—*Chicago Sun Times*

OTHER TITLES AVAILABLE FROM SAMUEL FRENCH

THE CURATE SHAKESPEARE AS YOU LIKE IT

Don Nigro

Comedy / 4m, 3f / Bare stage

This unusual piece is subtitled "The record of one company's attempt to perform the play by William Shakespeare". When the prolific Mr. Nigro was asked by a professional theatre company to adapt As You Like It so that it could be performed by a company of seven, he devised a completely original play about a rag tag group of players led by a dotty old curate who must present Shakespeare's play. The dramatic interest and the comedy derive from their hilarious attempts to impersonate all of Shakespeare's characters. The play has had numerous productions nationwide and has become an underground comic classic

OTHER TITLES AVAILABLE FROM SAMUEL FRENCH

WILLIAM SHAKESPEARE'S A MIDSUMMER NIGHT'S DREAM

Adapted by Everett Quinton

Comedy / 10m, 5f / Interior, Exterior

The Ridiculous Theatrical Company's version of A Midsummer Night's Dream is the magical story of star crossed lovers, overly ambitious homespun clowns and misadventures with the fairies. The fun can be multiplied by mixing and matching the male/female roles. The action begins at the beautiful court of Theseus, Duke of Athens, and later moves to the mystical forest inhabited by Oberon and Titania, king and queen of the fairies. And don't forget Puck fairyland was never like this!